# Jakers!™

# Piggley Makes a Pie

adapted by Wendy Wax
images by Entara Ltd.

Ready-to-Read

Simon Spotlight
New York    London    Toronto    Sydney

Based on the TV series *Jakers! The Adventures of Piggley Winks* created by Entara Ltd.

SIMON SPOTLIGHT
An imprint of Simon & Schuster Children's Publishing Division
1230 Avenue of the Americas, New York, New York 10020

Manufactured in the United States of America
First Edition
2 4 6 8 10 9 7 5 3 1
Library of Congress Cataloging-in-Publication Data
Wax, Wendy.
Piggley makes a pie / by Wendy Wax.— 1st ed.
p. cm. — (Ready-to-read. Level 1)
"Based on the TV series Jakers! The Adventures of Piggley Winks."
Summary: When Piggley and his friends eat more than their share of pie, they try to make a new one to cover up their greediness.
ISBN-13: 978-0-689-87613-4  ISBN-10: 0-689-87613-0
1. Rebuses. [1. Greed—Fiction. 2. Pies—Fiction. 3. Rebuses.] I. Title. II. Series.
PZ7.W35117Pi 2005
[E]—dc22
2004008591

**MRS. WINKS** made two

 **APPLE** **PIES** .

She put them by the  **WINDOW**

to cool.

"Would you like some  ?"
PIE

asked ![MRS. WINKS].
MRS. WINKS

"Yes, please," said ![PIGGLEY] ,
PIGGLEY

![FERNY] , ![DANNAN] , and ![MOLLY] .
FERNY    DANNAN    MOLLY

They ate the whole ![PIE] .
PIE

 asked for more 🥧 .

PIGGLEY                              PIE

"Not now," said 🐷 .

MRS. WINKS

"You can have some later."

Then she went to the store.

"That  smells good,"

PIE

said .

PIGGLEY

"But we cannot eat it now,"

said 🐷.

MOLLY

" 🐷 said no," said 🦆.

MRS. WINKS          DANNAN

"We can have a small taste,"

said  .

PIGGLEY

"Yes!" said  .

FERNY

"A small taste."

Soon the  was gone!

PIE

"Oh, no!" said  .

DANNAN

"We ate the whole  !

PIE

 will be mad."

MRS. WINKS

"We can make a new ," 
PIE

said .
PIGGLEY

"We need , , ,
APPLES      SUGAR      FLOUR

, and ."
EGGS            MILK

The friends took a
PAIL

to the   .
APPLE TREE

They tried to pick  .
APPLES

"I see a  !" said  .
GOAT     DANNAN

"Maaaaa," said the  .
GOAT

"He wants ," said  .
APPLES              FERNY

"I am scared," said  .
MOLLY

 put the on his head.

PIGGLEY          PAIL

He tried to scare the .

GOAT

The was not scared.

GOAT

" 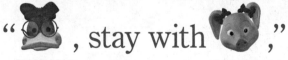, stay with ,"

DANNAN          MOLLY

said .

PIGGLEY

" , come with me."

FERNY

Soon another  came by.
GOAT

It was not a real  .
GOAT

It was  and  !
PIGGLEY          FERNY

The real  watched them
GOAT

pick  .
APPLES

Then they ran

back to the  .
HOUSE

"Mom will be home soon,"

said .

PIGGLEY

"We need to make the ."

PIE

Oops!  spilled the SUGAR!

PIGGLEY                    SUGAR

DANNAN got the EGGS.

FERNY got the MILK.

MOLLY got the FLOUR.

 and went all over ,

SUGAR　　　FLOUR　　　　　　　　　　PIGGLEY

, , and .

FERNY　　DANNAN　　　　MOLLY

"What a mess!" said .

PIGGLEY

"Your mom is here!"

said .

FERNY

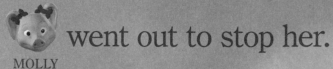 went out to stop her.

MOLLY

She did not want

MRS. WINKS

to see the mess.

PIGGLEY FERNY , and DANNAN

cleaned up the mess.

They used a

BROOM

and a .

SPONGE

Then they made a .

PIE

put in .

PIGGLEY          EGGS

put in and .

FERNY          SUGAR          FLOUR

put in .

DANNAN          MILK

They all put in .

APPLES

"Yuck!" said .

DANNAN

"This does not look good,"

said .

PIGGLEY

wished he had waited

PIGGLEY

to eat his mom's .

PIE

Next time he would do as

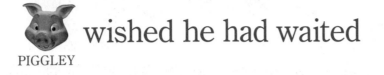 asked.

MRS. WINKS

 and  came in.

MRS. WINKS　　　MOLLY

 saw the new .

MRS. WINKS　　　　　PIE

She gave everyone .

FORKS

"Time to eat !"

PIE

she said with a smile.